Toast Mortem

Claudia Bishop

BERKLEY PRIME CRIME, NEW YORK

THE BERKLEY PUBLISHING GROUP
Published by the Penguin Group
Penguin Group (USA) Inc.
375 Hudson Street, New York, New York 10014, USA
Penguin Group (Canada), 90 Eglinton Avenue East, Suite 700, Toronto, Ontario M4P 2Y3, Canada
(a division of Pearson Penguin Canada Inc.)
Penguin Books Ltd., 80 Strand, London WC2R 0RL, England
Penguin Group Ireland, 25 St. Stephen's Green, Dublin 2, Ireland (a division of Penguin Books Ltd.)
Penguin Group (Australia), 250 Camberwell Road, Camberwell, Victoria 3124, Australia
(a division of Pearson Australia Group Pty. Ltd.)
Penguin Books India Pvt. Ltd., 11 Community Centre, Panchsheel Park, New Delhi—110 017, India
Penguin Group (NZ), 67 Apollo Drive, Rosedale, North Shore 0632, New Zealand
(a division of Pearson New Zealand Ltd.)
Penguin Books (South Africa) (Pty.) Ltd., 24 Sturdee Avenue, Rosebank, Johannesburg 2196,
South Africa

Penguin Books Ltd., Registered Offices: 80 Strand, London WC2R 0RL, England

TOAST MORTEM

A Berkley Prime Crime Book / published by arrangement with the author

PRINTING HISTORY
Berkley Prime Crime mass-market edition / June 2010

ISBN: 978-0-425-23028-2

BERKLEY® PRIME CRIME
Berkley Prime Crime Books are published by The Berkley Publishing Group,
a division of Penguin Group (USA) Inc.,
375 Hudson Street, New York, New York 10014.
BERKLEY® PRIME CRIME and the PRIME CRIME logo are trademarks of Penguin Group (USA) Inc.

PRINTED IN THE UNITED STATES OF AMERICA

10 9 8 7 6 5 4 3 2 1

For Lyn Stanton

Cast of Characters

The Inn at Hemlock Falls

Sarah "Quill" Quilliam-McHale . . . . *owner, manager*

Margaret "Meg" Quilliam . . . . *owner, master chef*

Jackson McHale . . . . *Quill's son*

Doreen Muxworthy-Stoker . . . . *housekeeper, a widow*

Dina Muir . . . . *receptionist and graduate student*

Kathleen Kiddermeister . . . . *head waitress*

Mike Santini . . . . *groundskeeper*

Nate . . . . *the bartender*

Elizabeth Chou . . . . *under chef*

Bjarne Bjarnsen . . . . *under chef*

Devon . . . . *dishwasher*

Mallory . . . . *dishwasher*

Max . . . . *dog*

Anson Fredericks . . . . *guest, member of WARP*

Muriel Fredericks . . . . *guest, his wife*

Verena Barbarossa . . . . *guest, president of WARP*

Big Buck Vanderhausen . . . . *guest, member of WARP*

William K. Collier. . . . . *guest, member of WARP*

And various waiters, waitresses, and housekeeping staff

The Hemlock Falls Chamber of Commerce

Elmer Henry . . . . *the mayor*

Adela Henry . . . . *his wife*

Marge Schmidt-Peterson. . . . . *local tycoon*

Harland Peterson. . . . . *dairy farmer, Marge's husband*

Howie Murchinson . . . . *judge and the village attorney*

Miriam Doncaster . . . . *librarian*

Harvey Bozzel. . . . . *advertising executive*

Reverend Dookie Shuttleworth . . . . *minister*

Esther West . . . . *owner, West's Best Kountry Krafts*

Nadine Peterson . . . . *owner, Hemlock Hall of Beauty*

And others

The Village of Hemlock Falls

Davy Kiddermeister . . . . *sheriff*

Carol Ann Spinoza . . . . *animal control officer*

Myles McHale. . . . . *Quill's husband, an investigator*

Justin Martinez . . . . *lawyer*

And various police officers, storekeepers, farmers, and citizens

Bonne Goutè Culinary Academy

Bernard Lévesque . . . . *famous chef, author of* Brilliance in the Kitchen

Madame LeVasque . . . . *his wife and chief financial officer*

Clarissa Sparrow . . . . *head pastry chef*

Raleigh Brewster . . . . *head of soups and stews*

Jim Chen . . . . *head chef, fish and seafood*

Pietro Giancava . . . . . . *head chef, sauces, chief sommelier*

Mrs. Owens . . . . *head chef, fruits and vegetables*

Bismarck . . . . *cat*

And various waiters, waitresses, and maintenance staff

Supernumeraries

Barstow and Phipps . . . . *LeVasque's lawyers*

Lieutenant Harker . . . . *a New York state trooper*

Prologue

Bernard LeVasque stormed into the kitchen at La Bonne Goutè Culinary Academy in his usual way: his left hand thrust palm out to smack open the swinging doors, his right clenched around his favorite butcher knife. "*Hola!* You collection of *stupides*!" he shouted, by way of greeting.

The academy's five chefs were assembled in the large, airy space.

Despite the fact that M. LeVasque had announced his presence in the same insulting tones for the past three months, all of them reacted with a range of very satisfying behaviors: Pietro Giancava (sauces and wines) hissed like a snake. Raleigh Brewster (soups and stews) let out a muffled shriek. Mrs. Owens (fruits and vegetables) growled like the mastiff she resembled. Jim Chen (seafood and fish) scowled, clenched his fists, and balanced himself evenly on both feet, as if readying to charge his employer.

The only person who remained unruffled was the young and pretty pastry chef, Clarissa Sparrow.

M. LeVasque was pretty sure he could fix that. Mme. Sparrow, he recalled, was the fond owner of Bismarck, the enormous orange-and-yellow cat glowering under the prep sink. Without a word, he strode across the terrazzo floor, grabbed Bismarck by the scruff of the neck, and flung the startled animal out the back door.

Then, with an insincere grin that bared his yellowing teeth, he said, *"Bon matin."*

1

~Courgettes et Tomates~
au Caviar LeVasque
For four personnes

2 medium tomatoes
2 small zucchini
Chopped onion
Chopped parsley
Caviar LeVasque*

Prepare the zucchini and vegetables by slicing in half and scooping out the seeds. Stuff with one cup Caviar LeVasque, garnish with parsley and onion, arrange beautifully.

*Caviar LeVasque is available at my website for a small fee only.

—From *Brilliance in the Kitchen*, B. LeVasque

"That Mr. Levaskew's going to end up with his butcher's knife buried smack in the middle of his back one of these days," Doreen Muxworthy-Stoker predicted. "You mark my words."

"Well, it won't be soon enough for me." Meg Quilliam sat curled in the lounge chair farthest away from the outer deck of the gazebo and bit her thumb with a cross expression. Her sister, Quill, sat on that part of the deck that faced the waterfall tumbling into Hemlock Gorge. Doreen, their housekeeper, perched on the sturdy gazebo railing like a broody hen. Jackson Myles McHale, who was going to be two years old in less than a week, climbed up the shallow steps to the gazebo floor and climbed back down again.

Quill kept a careful eye on her son and wriggled her bare toes in the soft moss that edged the decking.

It was a perfect August afternoon. Sunshine flooded the emerald green lawns surrounding the Inn at Hemlock Falls. Roses and lavender scented the soft air. Flowering clematis, shouting crimson, climbed over the old stone walls of the sprawling building. The breeze that came up from the gorge was cool and smelled of fresh water. Quill didn't want to talk about the horrible Mr. LeVasque. She wanted to roll over in the grass with Jack and tickle him until he collapsed into giggles. But she was a loyal friend and loving sister, so she said: "What's he done now?"

"What's he *done*?" Meg shrieked. "What hasn't he *done*!? He's built a whacking huge cooking academy smack in my backyard and stolen all our customers and you're asking me what's he *done*?!" She wriggled out of the lounge chair, put her hands on her hips, and glared across the gorge.

La Bonne Goutè Academy of Culinary Arts sat on the opposite side of the ravine. It was three stories high. Practically everyone in the village of Hemlock Falls thought it was gorgeous. The building was cream of cream clapboard with hunter green trim. The roof was smooth copper. All three stories were surrounded by clear pine decking. The place was surrounded by apple trees, peach trees, figs, and a vegetable garden that looked as if it belonged outside a French chateau with an army of gardeners at the *duc's* command.

Quill had gone to the open house three months before. Like all the other villagers in Hemlock Falls, she hadn't been able to keep away. She knew that the inside was as serviceable and elegant as the outside. The floors were wide-planked cedar, buffed to a perfect shine. The tasting room was big and dark and cool, and the antique wine racks that covered the walls had come from M. LeVasque's own vineyards in France. As for the kitchens . . . Quill sighed. The biggest classroom had twenty dual-fuel Viking ranges. Four were arranged in each of five stations complete with prep sinks and all the knives, spatulas, graters, sieves, choppers, bowls, measuring cups, ladles, spoons, and whisks an aspiring student chef could ask for.

Hemlock Falls was pleased with the addition of all this glory to their picturesque cobblestone village. Its proprietor, M. Bernard LeVasque, was the author of the best-selling cookbook *Brilliance in the Kitchen*. His television show *The Master at Work* had a successful five-year run on network TV. He attracted tourists in droves.

"I'd like to bomb the place," Meg said through gritted teeth. "I'd like to dump a billion tons of cow manure on that copper roof. I'd like to throw five hundred gallons of brindle brown paint all over that perfect siding."

Jackson Myles McHale glanced up at his aunt, a slight pucker between his feathery eyebrows. The sunshine made his red curls glow like a new penny. He seemed to debate a moment. Then he bent over, grabbed the red plastic shovel Quill had bought for him so he could dig in the dirt like Mike the groundskeeper, and presented it to Meg. "Frow this!" he said, with a pleased expression. "Frow it *now*."

"Thuh-row," Quill corrected gently. "Thuh-thuh-thuh. Thuh-row, Jack."

"Frow," Jack said ecstatically. "Frow, frow, frow!"

"Give it here, Jack," Meg demanded. "And I'll throw it right up M. LeVasque's . . ."

Quill cleared her throat noisily, then extracted the shovel from her son's chubby grasp and sat on it. "No throwing," she said firmly. "Either one of you. And M. LeVasque is undoubtedly a grouchy guy, Meg, but let's not talk about this kind of stuff in front of Jack, okay? And for God's sake, don't encourage him to throw things. You'll have to admit," she added, fondly, "that he's the smartest little boy and he picks up on everything."

"Phooey," Meg said.

"Phooey," Jack echoed. He made a determined effort to extract the shovel from beneath Quill's cotton skirt.

"There, you see?" Quill said. She held the shovel up in one hand. "Darling, you can only have the shovel if you promise not to throw it, okay?"

"Phooey," Jack said. He grabbed the shovel, gnawed at the handle for a bit, and threw the shovel down the steps.

Quill beamed at him. "Get the shovel and bring it back to Mommy, please."

"Phooey," Jack said. "Phooey-phooey-*phooey*!"

"That's enough, young man." Doreen jumped down from the railing and brushed herself off briskly. She wore her usual work uniform of denim skirt, cotton blouse, and canvas shoes. Her gray hair frizzed around her face and the tip of her nose was red from sunburn. Her hands and wrists were gnarled from arthritis and Quill marveled, as she occasionally did, at the toughness in her friend's wiry, seventy-eight-year-old frame. She'd outlived four husbands. Stoker, the last one, had died peacefully in his sleep and left Doreen a comfortably wealthy woman. "That's it. Nap time. Come here to Gram."

"Nap time," Jack said. "No. No. I don't think so."

Doreen bent over with a slight grunt of effort and picked him up. "Say night-night to Mommy." For a long moment, the two pairs of eyes regarded each other; Jack's bright blue and thoughtful, Doreen's black and beady. "Night-night, Gram," he said meekly. Then, suddenly, he yawned widely, put his head on Doreen's shoulder, and went to sleep.

"Amazing," Meg said. They watched the two of them cross the lawn to the Inn. With one hand supporting the toddler's back, Doreen opened the French doors to the Tavern Lounge and disappeared inside.

"It is, isn't it?" Quill sighed. "How come that never works for me?"

Meg turned her head. "You mean Jack and Doreen?" She scowled. "Because you turn into a sap every time you see him. He could stick beans up your nose and you'd think it's adorable. Doreen's over being a sap about kids. She's got how many grandchildren of her own?"

"Twenty-two, last count," Quill said. "And that includes Jack, she says. Furthermore, I am not a sap."

"Yes, you are," Meg fumed.

Quill decided not to argue the point. Her sister was the world's best fumer and she'd made it a long-standing practice to ignore the explosions.

Meg clasped her hands behind her back and began to pace. The gazebo was large. Its radius was twenty feet, which Quill knew because she'd designed it herself. And Meg was short, no more than five feet two, even when she was standing on her tiptoes in rage. But the place was too small to accommodate her sister's agitation.

"Here's an idea. Let's go to the beach."

Meg scowled at the gorge. It was a wonderful afternoon, warm, but not sticky, and the air coming up from the Hemlock River smelled like freshly cut grass. The water was a clear greeny brown. From where she stood in the gazebo, Quill could see it lapping peacefully against the little sandy beach she and Mike the groundskeeper had designed together and then installed that spring. Mike had built a sturdy pine staircase on the steep slopes that led down from the Inn, too. The whole thing was quite a hit with the guests. Quill was trying to encourage wisteria to grow around the railings. She'd planted several of the new hybrid hydrangeas at the foot of the stairs, and they were blooming like anything.

On the beach itself, which was small but smoothly sandy, two of the Inn's guests sunned themselves in the pair of Adirondack recliners. Both had sunhats over their faces, but from the brevity of the bikini on the one and the color of the Speedo on the other, it was Mr. and Mrs. Anson Fredericks.

"You mean go swimming? You're trying the change the subject. It's not going to work." Meg started to pace again, her gray eyes narrowed to tiny, glittering slits.

Quill had been trying to change the subject ever since the Bonne Goutè Culinary Academy had thrown open its oversized oak doors in April. Meg came back to it as if scratching at a case of poison ivy.

"You know how many bookings we've got for dinner tonight?"

Three, Quill said silently.

"Three!" Meg roared.

Far down the slope of Hemlock Gorge, Mrs. Fredericks sat up, looked around in a dissatisfied way, and poked her husband in the stomach.

"And it's the *height* of the tourist season. Last year at this time, do you know how many bookings we had the ninth of July?"

Forty-six, Quill said to herself.

"Forty-six!"

Quill sighed.

"And don't you dare try and tell me it's the economy!" Meg stamped to a halt and raised her fists over her head. "If God and the twelve apostles drove up to the Inn in a bus and wanted a room, what would we have to tell him?"

We're full.

"We're *full up!*" Meg flung herself into the wicker rocker next to the little refrigerated bar and pushed herself back and forth with a furious foot. "Oh, no," she said bitterly. "People are coming in droves to the Inn. You and Dina have to beat them off with a stick. But they're not coming for my food. They hate my food. They hate my recipes. They hate me! But the food made by that little jumped up pompous French son of a bi . . ."

Mrs. Fredericks shrieked. It wasn't her breakfast shriek. ("Oh, ew! This is cream? Do you know what kind of fat content is in cream? Don't you people have any soy? Ew!") Or her allergy shriek. ("Oh, ew! Do you know what roses *do* to my sinuses? Ew!")

This was a shriek of terror.

Quill crossed the short distance to the head of the beach staircase in two leaps and was halfway down its length before she pulled herself up and assessed the situation.

Mrs. Fredericks teetered precariously on her Adirondack chair. She waved her hat frantically at a fine, healthy clump of hydrangea. Anson Fredericks had backed into the water. He faced the clump of hydrangea, too. Quill was on the other side of the hydrangea, and from this vantage point, she could see a long, furry orange tail, a plump set of furry orange hindquarters, and two furry ears. The ears were pinned flat against a round hairy head. An ominous, continuous growl had replaced the cheery sound of birdsong.

It was a cat. A very large cat, and it had a bright red bandanna tied around its neck.

Quill started down the steps again.

The hindquarters bunched and the muscles under the glossy coat rippled. Mrs. Fredericks shrieked, "Anson! It's going to jump me!"

After ten years as an innkeeper, Quill was an expert soother. "It's just a cat, Mrs. Fredericks. You can't see him, her, whatever, from here. But I can, and it's just somebody's pet."

"Cat, my ass!" Muriel Fredericks screamed. "It's a goddam panther."

"Bring a gun!" Anson shouted. "We need some kind of gun!"

"A gun?" Quill said, startled.

"Don't move, Muriel! It's probably rabid!" Anson splashed a few feet farther into the river.

Muriel teetered on the edge of the chair and regarded her husband with undisguised contempt. "A fat lot you care, you, you *coward*."

"It's not going to jump," Quill soothed.

The animal crouched, and its already flattened ears flattened some more. It wriggled its belly into the mulch and flexed its long, sharp claws.

"And if it's going to jump, it's because you're waving your hat around. It thinks you're inviting him to play."

Quill reached the bottom of the steps and regarded the cat a little dubiously. It looked very much like a well-fed domestic tabby except it was much, much, larger. Quill had a good visual sense, and the thing had to weigh forty pounds, at least. "Here, kitty," she said. "Here, kitty, kitty."

"That there's a Maine coon cat." Doreen's voice came from just behind Quill's left ear. She turned around to see that the cavalry had arrived in the form of her sister and her housekeeper. "A what?"

"A Maine coon cat," Doreen explained patiently. "It's one of them big ones."

"It sure is," Meg said, somewhat awed.

The cat turned and regarded the three of them with the sort of confident imperiousness Quill tried to cultivate with her more obnoxious guests. (It never worked.) It growled, drew its lips back over very sharp teeth, and spat. Then it sat up and began to wash its tail with the kind of complete indifference Quill tried to cultivate with cranky food inspectors. (That never worked, either.)

"Well!" Quill said brightly. "You see? It's quite relaxed now that you've stopped waving the hat. I think everything's going to be just fine, Mrs. Fredericks. We've got this under control. Why don't you and your husband go back up to the Inn and relax for a bit in the Tavern Lounge." She looked at her watch. "It's five-ish. You'll be just in time for a nice high tea. Tell Nate the bartender that there'll be no charge."

"More like time for a double martini," Anson Fredericks said as he edged past them.

"Yeah," Muriel said, as she followed him. "And we're due at Bonne Goutè for the Wine Fest at seven. I don't want to spoil it. I think you owe us a few drinks, if you ask me. All that cream and scones stuff is fattening. Not to mention bad for your arteries."

Quill was pretty sure the growling sound wasn't coming from the cat but from her sister, although it was hard to tell. She took a firm grip on Meg's arm and pulled her off the steps and onto the sand. "Martinis, then. Whatever you like."

She didn't watch the Frederickses go but tried to keep a wary eye on both her sister and the cat at the same time, which was difficult, since the cat had retreated farther under the hydrangea. Meg was at the water's edge, throwing fist-sized rocks into the water in a petulant way.

Doreen pushed past Quill, crouched a few feet away from the hydrangea bush and extended her hand. "C'mere, you."

The cat, its front paws folded under its substantial chest, stared at them with the arrogance of a homeboy defending his turf from punks the next street over.

"C'mere, cat." Doreen opened her right hand, which held a revolting-looking gray brown mush. The cat sniffed, sat up, and started to purr like a lawnmower. Then it daintily picked its way through the mulch surrounding the hydrangea and swiped at Doreen's hand. Doreen hollered, dropped the mush, and backed away. The cat smirked and considered the mush. Then it ate it.

"What *is* that stuff?" Quill demanded.

"Liver bits."

"Liver bits?" Quill took a minute to process this. "You carry liver around in your pockets?"

"Jack likes it."

"You feed Jack liver?!"

"Sure."

"Doreen! Liver's an organ meat. It's filled with choles-
terol. It's stuffed with fat. It's horrible stuff."

"A-yuh." Doreen scowled at the cat and looked at the
scratch on her hand, which oozed a small bit of blood.

"I don't want you to feed Jack liver bits ever again. Do
you hear me?"

Doreen ignored this, as she ignored most of Quill's frequent caveats about the care of her son. "What are we going
to do with this here cat?"

"If it were Thanksgiving instead of weeks after the
Fourth of July, I could stuff it like a turkey," Meg said. She
tossed a final handful of rocks into the river and dusted her
hands on her shorts. "It's big enough to feed sixteen."

The cat narrowed its eyes chillingly.

"Just kidding," Meg said. She crouched next to Doreen.
"What are we going to do with it? It's too big to tote up the
stairs, that's for sure."

"We could call animal control," Quill suggested ner-
vously.

Everybody ignored this, including the cat. Quill was
sorry she'd brought it up. The recently appointed animal
control officer was Carol Ann Spinoza, who had lost her
cushy job as the village of Hemlock Falls' meanest tax as-
sessor and was now the village's meanest dog catcher.

"We'll put up a notice in the post office," Quill said.
"And maybe your friend Arthur can publish its picture in
the *Gazette*, Doreen, if that's okay with you. It's obviously
somebody's pet."

They all looked at the red bandanna, which was neatly
ironed and carefully tied.

"And I'm sure that its owner is searching frantically for
it," Quill added.

Meg looked dubious. Quill wasn't too sure of it, herself. But Doreen nodded and scooped another handful of liver bits from her pocket. The cat looked up at her with calculating interest and came out into the sunshine.

"And we'll bring food down for it, that's what we'll do." Quill pulled her cell phone from her pocket. Myles had given her a new one at Christmas and she'd painfully learned all the applications, so she could take pictures of Jack to send to his father. Myles had been on assignment in the Middle East for four months, and if she stopped to think about it, she couldn't bear it. So she took picture after picture and texted them off, and it helped, a little, but not really enough. She peered through the little viewfinder and said, "Can you guys move him away from the flowers?"

"Not me," Meg said flatly. "He's still mad about the turkey comment."

Doreen laughed scornfully and sucked the scratch mark on the palm of her hand.

"Never mind, then." Quill backed up a few feet. "I'm just trying to compose a better shot. The thing is, that red bandanna looks positively dire with that orange coloring, and the whole thing clashes with the blue hydrangea." The silence was marked. Quill looked up from the viewfinder. "What?!"

"Just take the shot," Meg said. "Yes, you are an artist. And yes, you've got an oil hanging at MoMA. And yes, countless critics have applauded your—what was the phrase in *Art Today*? Your preternatural sense of color. But."

"But?"

"That cat's a menace," Doreen said. "We gotta get the word out, or next thing you know it's going to be eating the guests. If you don't take the picture, I will. Besides, that there bandanna might help with identification." She snorted. "And who's going to give a rat's behind about the color of them hydrangeas?"

"I don't know if the bandanna's going to make all that much difference. That's a one-of-a-kind cat, that is," Meg observed.

"Will you guys stand next to it, then? I need a reference point so people can see how big it is."

Meg flatly refused, on the grounds that the cat would just as soon bite her as look at her. Doreen didn't bother to reply to this suggestion at all, although she scattered some of the liver bits under the bush to tempt the animal farther into the sunshine.

Meg clicked her tongue impatiently. "Come on, Quill. Hurry up. I've got to get to the kitchen and prep for all three of the stupendous meals I'm making tonight. And you've got that executive session for the Chamber of Commerce at five o'clock, don't you?"

Guiltily, Quill looked at her watch again. She'd be late for the executive session. She sighed, moved the cell phone up and down and crosswise, and shot five really bad photos of the cat. Then she took the rake they always left by their little beach and neatened the sand up and they all trooped back up the stairs.

~

Bismarck ate the rest of the liver bits. He stretched, yawned widely, and retired under the hydrangea bush to plot revenge against the Frenchman.

2

~Asperes Vinaigrette~
For four personnes

16 stalks young asparagus
Vinaigrette LeVasque*

Poach the asparagus lightly in salted water. Drain.
Arrange beautifully on plates. Dribble the Vinaigrette
LeVasque over the stalks in an attractive way. Eat
with the fingers, *non*?

*Vinaigrette LeVasque is available at my website for a
small fee only.*

—From *Brilliance in the Kitchen*, B. LeVasque

Marge Schmidt-Peterson squinted at the tiny picture of the
cat on Quill's cell phone and shook her head. "Don't think
I've seen it around. It's a big sucker, though." Marge, a
local businesswoman, and the richest person in Tompkins
County, was the Chamber treasurer. She passed the camera
on to Elmer Henry.

Elmer, mayor of Hemlock Falls and current president of
the Hemlock Falls Chamber of Commerce, took a long,
earnest look and said, "I do believe I have seen that animal
somewhere."

"Really?" Quill said hopefully. She was the Chamber secretary and, due to a certain amount of absentmindedness when it came to taking notes, not a very good one. She was reelected each year under protest. Hers.

"Can't bring it to mind, though." He passed the camera on to Harland Peterson, a local dairy farmer who'd been elected vice president because Marge Schmidt-Peterson had married him last year, and she wanted it that way. Harland was chewing a toothpick. He shifted the toothpick from one side of his mouth to the other and said, "We got a calf about the size of that thing, Margie. But none of 'em are missing, as far as I know."

"Cat or no cat, we got to get down to business," Elmer said briskly.

"Right," Marge said, with a heavy emphasis that didn't bode well for a fast-moving meeting. "It's about those damn parking meters in front of my restaurants."

Elmer sighed. "We've been over this before, Marge. The board of supervisors voted 'em in, and they're going to stay right where they are."

"You know how many of my customers are bellyaching about those meters?"

"I know," he said huffily, "because you keep calling my office and bellyaching about them yourself. All I have to say to you is that they're bringing much-needed income to this town, and anyone who complains about helping those kids out at the high school . . ."

"Who's complaining about helping the kids at the high school?"

"You are! Those parking meter funds can be used for extra textbooks, extra computers, what have you."

"Could be? Or actually are?"

Elmer hunched his shoulders. "Soon. Anyways, you're just a plain bad citizen, Marge, to take textbooks away from the hands of those high schoolers. Besides," he added, "it isn't all that much, when you come right down to it. You got a bunch of cheapskates there at your diner, Marge. Not my fault if they aren't willing to part with a few quarters to eat at your place."

"Textbooks," Marge repeated.

"They can be used for that, yes, sir." Elmer's sigh would have done credit to Saint Sebastian facing the arrows. After a short—and on Marge's part, disconcerted, silence—he waved the official gavel, and finding nowhere convenient to whack it, shifted grumpily in his chair. "How come we're squashed in here like this, Quill?"

Quill's office was located just past the front door to the Inn, behind the reception desk. When it was occupied by three comfortably sized citizens of Hemlock Falls, it seemed to have too much furniture. Marge and Harland sat together on the three-cushioned couch, which was patterned in heavy chintz printed with bronze chrysanthemums. Quill sat behind her desk, which was made of cherry and in the Queen Anne style. Elmer sat at the small Queen Anne table, which was totally covered by the coffee service and a plate of Meg's sour cream scones.

"I'm sorry it's a little crowded," Quill said. "The group we have here booked the conference room every day this week."

"They got a meeting at five o'clock in the afternoon?" Elmer said. "I saw most of 'em in the Tavern Lounge knocking back booze when I came in. If they're not meeting in there right this minute why are we stuck in this place?"

"They don't want anyone in there," Quill said. "Not even the cleaning staff. They lock it when they aren't inside."

Marge pursed her lips. "What kind of group would that be?"

Quill hesitated. Marge generally put people in mind of one of those short, aggressive tanks that had been so successful in Iraq (although marriage to Harland had mellowed her a bit), which made ducking her interrogations somewhat hazardous. "It's called WARP."

"WARP?"

"Like *Star Trek*," Quill said, somewhat obscurely.

"It's some kind of rehab program," Elmer said. "One of those twelve-step jobbers."

Quill blinked. She thought about asking Elmer why in the world he thought that, but didn't. Everybody had what they thought was an informed opinion in a town the size of Hemlock Falls.

"Drunks," Elmer said comprehensively. "And you let 'em in the Tavern bar?"

"They aren't drunks," Marge said. "They don't look like drunks or act like drunks. And even if they were drunks, it's none of your business, Elmer."

Quill, who thought that drinkers came in all shapes and sizes and couldn't be pigeonholed, had to agree that it wasn't anyone's business whether the WARP people drank all the gin in Tompkins County. Although if WARP's bar bill was anything to go by, it had to be the most unsuccessful twelve-step program ever.

Marge pinned Quill with a steely gaze. "Looks like they got quite a bit of money to throw around. Why don't you bring them on down to the Croh Bar for Happy Hour sometime this week?"

"Insurance business is a bit slow," Harland said, by way of explanation. "Margie's not one to pass up a good prospect."

"Oh. Well." Quill cleared her throat. Marge was perfectly capable of marching down the hallway to the Tavern Lounge and shaking Big Buck Vanderhausen by the scruff of the neck until he coughed up a premium on his dually. "When the organizers booked the rooms, they stressed the confidential nature of their group," she said apologetically. "And they especially asked about how private we were here at the Inn." Then, because she wasn't certain what she had to apologize for, she added firmly, "I'm not sure that it's a recovery program. They seem to be interested in small business. They asked me to give them a talk on how to run a bed-and-breakfast, for example."

"This isn't a bed-and-breakfast," Marge said with a dangerous look in her eye. "And if they want to know anything about running a small business, why didn't you tell them about me?"

"You don't want to talk about business with a bunch of drunks," Elmer said patiently.

"They aren't drunks," Quill said.

"Kayla Morrison found the Serenity Prayer in a wastebasket in that room two-twenty-five of yours," Elmer said. "Told me so herself."

Kayla was a new hire in housekeeping and clearly needed a reminder about the innkeeper's number one rule: no gossiping. Although, come to think of it, not gossiping wasn't as important as not belting the guests, so it'd have to be the number two rule.

"Serenity Prayer. Rehab. Stands to reason," Harland said thoughtfully. "Drunks, huh?"

"I wouldn't call the existence of the Serenity Prayer any kind of evidence at all, Elmer. Lots of people find the Serenity Prayer very soothing."

Elmer looked smug. "Drunks, for example."

"Look at the Irish," Quill said. "You'll find a copy of that prayer in every pub in Ireland."

"Like I said. Dru . . ."

"Shut up, Elmer," Marge said. "We've got enough troubles without you insulting the Irish. You planning on getting this meeting going anytime soon?"

"I have enough trouble with you insulting *me*," Elmer said, with a certain amount of dignity.

The meeting descended into a squabble, a regular Chamber practice, and Quill drifted into a brief reverie.

The precise nature of the WARP group puzzled her a little, if only because none of the members were at all alike. A recovery program was a reasonable explanation for the wildly disparate personalities, so Elmer might be half right. The very urban Fredericks huddled in earnest conversation with Mrs. Barbarossa (seventy-two and a cross-stitching grandmother), who in turn spent most mornings with Big Buck Vanderhausen from Lubbock, Texas (forty-six and an expert in long-haul trucking). And then there was the odiously unctuous mortgage banker William Knight Collier, who had an *America for Americans!* sticker on his car. What all these people had in common she couldn't imagine.

"Anyway!" Elmer whacked the gavel on the table leg. "I call this executive session of the Hemlock Falls Chamber of Commerce meeting to order. And if you can keep your opinions to yourself for a change, Marge Schmidt, I'd appreciate it."

"Peterson," Marge barked.

"Huh?"

Marge tapped the very large diamond on her ring finger with an admonitory air.

"Yeah, well. Whatever. Quill? You got the minutes from the last meeting?"

Quill gave a guilty start and patted the side pockets of her skirt. She pulled out her sketch pad (which was filled with charcoal drawings of Jack), a couple of tissues, the flash card for her cell phone, and a small tube of sunscreen. No minutes. She tugged at her hair and thought a minute. Since Myles's assignment overseas was to last six months or more, she had moved out of their small cobblestone house and back into her old suite on the third floor of the Inn. She was pretty sure the minutes were on top of Jack's clean diapers upstairs. Or maybe not.

"We don't need the minutes," Marge said, after a swift appraisal of Quill's thoughtful face. "This is an executive session, and we're here to approve the budget for the Welcome Dinner. We only need the minutes if we've got a full chamber meeting, and this isn't it."

"Lucky for us," Elmer grumbled. "We'd be squashed like sardines if the full Chamber was to meet in here."

Quill flipped to a clean page in her sketch pad. "Ready!" she said brightly.

"Finally!" Elmer said. "Okay, Margie. What we have is this amazing chance to offer a great big welcome to the best thing that's hit this town since I don't know what."

"Since the Colonel Cluck's Fried Chicken hut, maybe?" Marge asked sarcastically. "Or maybe MacAvoy's famous nudie bar? Or the Church of the Rolling Moses?"

These references to past civic disasters failed to ruffle Elmer's spirits. "I mean the Bon Gooty culinary place," he said patiently. "You missed the last Chamber meeting, on account of Harland's cows calving all at once, but we decided to give M'ser LeVasque a hearty how-do at Chamber expense." (Under stress, Elmer's Kentucky origins were obvious in his speech.)

Marge rolled a startled eye in Quill's direction. "We did?"

"We did," Quill said. "Since the culinary academy opened up, tourist revenues have gone up by . . . by . . ." She flipped through the sketch pad, in fruitless search for her notes on the exact percentage. "By a lot," she finished.

"The man's a genius." Elmer's expression of solemn respect nettled Marge, who grunted in a derisive way. But she said, reluctantly, "You might be right about that. He's got out-of-towners flocking to that place. And when we get tourists, everyone benefits. I hear the resort's booked through the summer. The Marriott down on Route 15 is doing well, too." She swiveled her head and eyed Quill. "Even you guys are full up these days. And it's all students and people wanting to slurp down wine and stuff their faces with this so-called gourmet food at Bernie's academy." She sucked reflectively on her lower lip. "Both my restaurants are doing okay, too, despite those damn parking meters. People's guts

need a rest from the fancy stuff." Marge's partner, Betty
Hall, was in charge of both the All-American Diner (Fine
Food! And Fast!) and the popular Croh Bar. Meg claimed
that Betty was the best short-order cook in the eastern
United States.

"Exactly," Elmer said. "Everybody's doing right well by
this fellow."

Marge's steely gaze narrowed a touch. "Except Meg.
Way I hear it, you got people stayin' here at the Inn, but
they ain't eating here at the Inn."

Nobody looked at Quill.

"Yeah," Elmer said. "Well, that's true. The way I see it,
there's a limit to how much gourmet food a body can take.
You've got to take the bitter with the sweet, I always say.
Anyhow!" He thumped the gavel against the chair leg, but
since everyone in the room was paying attention to him
already, it seemed quite superfluous to Quill, who was
smarting a little at the cavalier dismissal of her sister's con-
cerns. "So here's the thing. We're giving M'ser LeVasque a
thank-you from the town this Friday."

"How much of a thank-you?" Marge asked.

Elmer addressed the air over his head. "Hello? Excuse
me? Is this why we're having an executive session here?"
He lowered his gaze and looked just past Marge, concentrating on the oil painting hanging over the couch. Quill had
painted it twelve years ago, just after she and Meg had purchased the Inn. The two sisters sat on the banks of the gorge,
with the waterfall behind them. "I just got the numbers from
M'ser LeVasque, and all we have to do is vote approval of
the budget . . ."

Marge leaned forward and clapped a meaty hand on Elmer's thigh. "Hang on a second. You got numbers from
who? And for what?"

"A select dinner of the town's most important officials."
Elmer slipped an envelope out of his shirt pocket. "LeVasque

says he won't cook for more than thirty people, though. So we have to keep the invite list pretty quiet. I got the menu and the budget right here." He waved the envelope in the air. Marge grabbed it, removed the contents, smoothed it out on her knee. She looked up at Elmer and glowered.

There was a short silence.

"This would be you and Adela, attending this here dinner," Marge said. Something in the tone of her voice reminded Quill of the very aggressive cat under the hydrangea bush outside.

Elmer nodded. "And you and Harland, of course, and Howie and Miriam."

"The town justice and the village librarian," Marge said. Since everyone in the room knew perfectly well who Howie Murchison and Miriam Doncaster were, Quill knew Marge was making a point. But where Marge was headed was anybody's guess.

"Who else?" Marge demanded. "Dookie and them?"

Quill fiddled with her pencil. Then she started a quick sketch of a scowling Marge holding a panicked Elmer upside down by his heels. When Marge's grammar started to deteriorate, you knew she was annoyed.

"Of course, the Reverend and Mrs. Shuttleworth will be invited," Elmer said. "Most of the Chamber members. Thing is, he won't cook for more than thirty people, being a particular person, so we won't be able to have all of the Chamber members there."

"That's it?"

"That's it."

"We've got twenty-four members, and that doesn't count the spouses. How are you picking and choosing?"

Elmer ran a finger under his shirt collar. "We have to decide that at this meeting. I was thinking that maybe you . . ."

Marge's laugh was exactly like a pistol shot. "I'm supposed

to pick out nine Chamber members and tell them we're spending a ton of town money for a dinner by the best chef in the United States of America and they ain't invited?"

"Well," Elmer said feebly.

"And where is this banquet supposed to go on?"

"At Bonne Goutè, of course."

Marge hunched forward, forearms on her knees, her teeth inches from Elmer's face. "I'm looking at a bill that's a hundred dollars a plate for thirty people. And that don't include the drinks. Who's paying for this, Elmer?"

"The town, of course," Elmer said. "You know how much money we're making from those parking meters?"

3

~Confiture de Tomates Rouge~

6 pounds medium-sized red tomatoes
4½ pounds finely ground sugar
Zest of lemon rind plus juice

Slice tomatoes, remove seeds, slice thinly, and arrange in large glass bowl. Sprinkle sugar attractively over all. Let sit for twenty-four hours. Cook over low heat for two hours after adding lemon seasoning. Cool. Spoon into sterilized jars and label.*

*Your personalized home-cooking jar labels may be purchased from my website.
> —From *Brilliance in the Kitchen*, B. LeVasque

"What was the ruckus out front half an hour ago?" Meg stood at the birch prep table in her big kitchen, a cleaver in one hand and a clump of cilantro in the other. "Somebody get attacked by bees?"

"Marge got mad at the mayor." Quill settled into the rocking chair by the cobblestone fireplace and propped her feet up on the cast-iron fender. "And then the mayor got mad at Marge. And then Harland Peterson settled it by yelling the loudest. And then everyone went home."

"That was all the car doors slamming." Meg began whacking the cilantro into little pieces. "Now, in better times"—whack!—"I couldn't have heard a thing"—whack!—"because my kitchen would be full of the happy sound of two sous-chefs prepping for dinner, the pot person scrubbing pots, and the bus person scrubbing the sinks." Whack! Whack! Whack! "But, as you can see, I'm here in glory all by my silent lonesome." She scooped up the bits and dropped them into a stainless-steel bowl. Then she folded her arms and glared at her sister.

Quill set the rocker going with a shove of her foot. "At least we didn't have to lay anyone off. We're always full for breakfast. And lunches aren't too bad. And the dishwasher and the prep person will be in pretty soon."

"How long do you think Bjarne and Elizabeth are going to hang around making scrambled eggs and rye toast?"

Both sous-chefs had been with Meg for years, and were fiercely jealous of the Inn's reputation. They were even fiercer about their own reputations in the notoriously competitive world of gourmet cooking.

Meg correctly interpreted Quill's look of dismay. "They're professionals, for cripes's sake. They need a challenge. And don't even *hint* that breakfast can be as difficult as dinner."

"Lunch . . ." Quill ventured.

"Hah. Lunch is day-trippers and campers wanting macaroni and cheese."

This was true. Quill cast a wistful look around the kitchen. The twelve-burner Viking stove was polished to its usual brilliant sheen. A twelve-gallon pot of water simmered on one of the back burners, with a comfortably familiar sound. The herbs and spices hanging from the oak beams overhead scented the air with sage, thyme, and garlic. From her seat by the fireplace, she could see the vegetable garden out back, overflowing with early August bounty: tomatoes, green beans, cucumbers, onions, yellow squash, and manically over-productive zucchini. Meg had added edible flowers to her herb garden a few years back, and there was a glimpse of the bright orange reds of nasturtiums beyond the wire fence Mike had put up to keep out the rabbits. It was homey and beautiful. But it wasn't as slick as the kitchens and gardens at Bonne Goutè. It wasn't even close.

Meg grabbed a colander of ripe tomatoes, marched to the stove, and dumped the fruit into the pot.

"Gazpacho?" Quill guessed, hopefully.

"Maybe," Meg said crossly. "Maybe I'm getting them nice and soft so I can pitch them at Bernard LeVasque the next time he sets foot in my kitchen." She grabbed the pot, marched to the sink, and drained the tomatoes back into the colander. Then she began to peel them with her bare fingers. Meg's hands looked like most professional chefs'—calloused and scarred with knife cuts—but Quill still couldn't figure out why she never seemed to feel the heat of things like parboiled tomatoes. Then what Meg had just said registered and she said, "What? LeVasque's been in your kitchen?"

"Yep."

"When!"

"Just after lunch."

"Just after lunch?" At least that explained Meg's ill humor out in the gazebo. "And he's gone now?"

"Unless Mike ran him over in the kitchen parking lot."

Quill got up, went to the back door, which was open on this pleasant summer afternoon, and peered outside. All she saw was her dog, Max, stretched peacefully under the balcony that ran across the back of the building. The only cars in the lot were her battered Honda, Meg's old pickup truck, and a rusty Ford Escort that probably belonged to a friend of Mike the groundskeeper. She came back inside and tugged at her hair. Quill's hair was red and wildly springy and it suffered a lot from her emotional states. She perched on one of the stools at the prep station. "So tell me what happened."

"Offered me a job," Meg said briefly. "Figured I had some time on my hands and could use the extra work."

"Oh, my." Quill shot a glance at the wall where the sauté pans were neatly arrayed by size. The eight-incher was still in place and didn't seem to be dented. Meg usually chose the eight-incher when she was in the mood to make her point in a forceful way.

Meg followed her gaze and said, "Nope . . . I didn't chase him out of here with that."

"Then what?" Quill asked, rather hollowly.

Meg nodded at the knife rack. The largest butcher's cleaver hung slightly askew.

"Yikes," Quill said.

"That fathead," Meg said without heat. "Thought he'd come here to crow, but I fixed his little red wagon."

"You didn't actually hit him or anything," Quill said.

Meg rolled her eyes. "Have I ever, in all my life, actually inflicted physical harm on another person?"

"Bobby DeRitter, in fourth grade," Quill said promptly. "You pulled a fistful of hair right out of his tiny little head."

"Okay. Excepting Bobby DeRitter. Who deserved it, by the way."

"No," Quill admitted. "You throw stuff around. You holler. But I'd have to say, it's basically stress relief. So you just waved the butcher's cleaver at LeVasque."

"I may have given LeVasque a different impression," Meg admitted. "I may have intimated that the garden out back is the repository for a number of people who've incurred my disapproval, and I may have suggested that I was ready to add to their number."

"A-*hum*," Quill said.

"So we may be getting a visitor."

"A visitor?"

The screen door at the back slapped open and closed.

First in was Max, Quill's dog. If Tompkins County ever ran an ugly dog contest, Max would win hands down. His coat was mostly to blame for his raffish appearance. It was a strange mixture of gray, ochre, tan, scruffy white, and flecks of black. One ear flopped over his left eye. The other stood straight up. At some point in his bohemian past, he'd broken his plumelike tail, and it drooped in a desultory way over his hindquarters.

Behind Max was Davy Kiddermeister, the village sheriff. Quill was pretty sure that the clench in her stomach wasn't due to her need for some food, but to the official-looking document Davy held in his hand and the blush that turned his normally pink cheeks bright red. Davy was Kathleen Kiddermeister's younger brother. Kathleen was the Inn's most loyal waitress, and every time the Quilliam sisters ran afoul of the sheriff's department (a frequent occurrence, due mostly to Meg's and Quill's misguided efforts at amateur detection) Kathleen gave Davy what for. It looked like Davy was dreading his sister's wrath once again.

"Oh, dear," Quill said. "Just tell me nobody's dead."

"Nobody's dead. Somebody's pissed off, though. Sorry. But I've got to lay this on Meg, here." He waved the document in the air. When neither Quill nor Meg moved forward to take it, he straightened up, walked over to Meg, and said sternly, "Margaret Quilliam?"

"Phuut!" Meg said.

"I hereby serve you this summons and complaint." He grabbed her hand and folded her tomato-stained fingers over it. "Sorry about that. Sometimes it's rough, having to perform official duties. I know you won't hold it against me."

Meg shrugged. "Whatever."

He added hopefully, "Got anything to eat?"

"Give me that." Quill leaned over and grabbed the summons.

Meg relinquished the paper without comment. "Liver pâté with stone-ground mustard. And some pretty good goat salami." She moved to the meat refrigerator and took out a couple of plastic containers. "Some blueberries, maybe?"

"Thanks," Davy said gratefully. He eased himself onto a prep stool. "Been on traffic patrol all day and I missed lunch."

"This says you threatened to kill Bernard LeVasque," Quill said. "At least, I think that's what it says. *Threat of grievous bodily harm, assault* . . . battery is actually whacking somebody, right? Assault's the threat. So there's no allegation of actual injury. Thank goodness for that." She folded the paper into neat thirds. "Argh. Argh. I suppose I'd better call Howie Murchison."

"Got a warrant, too," Davy said through a mouthful of pâté. "Sorry."

"A warrant? For Meg's arrest?!"

"Yep. Sor—"

"Stop," Quill said. Then, patiently, she continued, "Did anyone actually see this alleged assault? I mean, if it's just Meg's word against LeVasque's, there's no independent proof."

"Yep."

"Please don't talk with your mouth full, Davy." There were many advantages to being the fond mother of a two-year-old. Chief among them was Quill's newly discovered ability to make polite demands. "And 'yep,' it's just LeVasque's unsubstantiated word, or 'yep,' there's a witness?"

The swinging doors to the dining room banged open, and Dina Muir, Quill's best (and only) receptionist walked in. She was followed by a slim, pretty brunette, who looked vaguely familiar.

Dina bent a purposeful eye on the platter of blueberries and headed over to the prep counter. "Hey, Quill. Hey, Meg." She gave Davy a pleased smile. "And what are you doing here? We're still on for the movies tonight, I hope?"

"Yep."

Quill resisted the impulse to yank the liver pâté away from Davy and dump it into the disposal, along with the fistful of blueberries Dina was cramming into her mouth.

Dina's long brown hair was drawn back in a jaunty ponytail. She adjusted her red-rimmed spectacles by resettling them on her nose with a forefinger and beamed. "Great. I've been looking forward to the movies all week. It's been a real zoo, here. Those WARP people must have robbed a bank somewhere, and they're trying to spend all their ill-gotten gains at once. Do you know what they're going to do tonight? They ordered *four* stretch limos from . . ."

Quill held up her hand. "Can we talk about this later? We have kind of a situation here." She smiled apologetically at the brunette, who looked anxious. "Hi! I'm Sarah Quilliam."

The brunette nodded and bit her lip. "I know. I mean, I've heard of you. You're the artist, right? I've seen some of your work at MoMA." She stuck out her hand. "I'm Clarissa Sparrow."

"I think I've seen you before," Quill said.

Clarissa looked even more anxious.

"But I can't quite . . ."

"We've got to go," Davy said abruptly. "Thanks for the lunch, Meg. It was great." He stood up and unclipped the handcuffs attached to his belt. "You ready?"

"For cripes' sake," Meg said. "You aren't serious."

"A warrant's a warrant," Davy said. "You give Howie a call, Quill, and we'll get her back on remand in no time, but like I said, we've got to go."

"This is not going to happen," Quill said firmly. "I am not allowing my sister to be dragged off to the county lockup by you or anyone else. For all you know, LeVasque could have made up this whole thing? Where's your proof that my sister threatened to kill him? Where's the witness?"

Davy jerked his thumb in Dina's direction.

Quill whirled and stared incredulously at Dina. Dina paled, bit her thumb, and said, "Oh my God."

"Don't you oh-my-God, me, Dina Muir! You told Davy you saw my sister threaten this bozo?"

"Um," Dina said.

"Um! That's all you've got to say for yourself! Um?!"

"I didn't think . . ."

"You most certainly did *not* think!"

"Oh my God," Dina repeated feebly.

Quill turned back to Davy, who had clipped one handcuff around Meg's wrist and was about to fasten the other. "You get those things off my sister!"

"Thing is," Davy said reasonably, "you can't expect someone like Meg to go quietly."

"She's not going anywhere!"

Davy sighed. "Look. I don't like this any better than you do. But what am I supposed to do here? I've got this warrant. A threat to commit grievous bodily harm is a major felony. I'm supposed to give you guys a break? No way, Quill. I'm sworn to uphold the law." He glanced sidelong at Quill's furious face and said pleadingly, "Now what do you suppose the sheriff would do?"

Clarissa spoke up suddenly. "I thought you were the sheriff."

"He means Myles," Quill said. "My husband. Myles was sheriff of Hemlock Falls when we moved here twelve years ago, and nobody seems to be able to forget it. Including you, Davy. Only now is when you should forget that you are. Sheriff, that is. As for what Myles would do." She grabbed her hair with both hands. "I would not let him arrest my sister!"

Davy gave Meg a gentle nudge toward the back door. "Call Mr. Murchison. As soon as I have a legal remand order, I'll bring her right back home. Okay?"

"Meg!" Quill shouted as her sister's slight form disappeared out the back door. "I'll be down to get you out in two seconds."

"Call up Bjarne!" Meg shouted back. "Tell him to save the tomatoes!"

4

~Carottes LeVasque~
For four personnes

2 pounds elegantly small carrots
4 tablespoons olive oil
⅔ cup water
4 tablespoons Paysanne LeVasque*
Parsley

Rinse, peel, and slice the carrots. Sauté in olive oil. Sprinkle with sea salt. Cook over low flame for ten minutes, shaking pan occasionally. Add my country spice mix (Paysanne LeVasque) and salt and pepper to taste. Cook covered for twenty minutes. Sprinkle attractively with parsley and serve warm.

Paysanne LeVasque may be purchased from my website.

—From *Brilliance in the Kitchen*, B. LeVasque

For a long moment, Clarissa Sparrow, Dina, and Quill just stood and looked at each other. The little impasse was broken by Max, who made an abortive lunge at the remains of the liver pâté on Davy's plate. Dina hauled him off the counter by the scruff of the neck.

"Just give me two seconds here," Quill said. She pulled her cell phone out of her pocket and found Howie Murchison's office number on speed dial. He wasn't in. She glanced up at the kitchen clock. Well after six o'clock. Doreen would be giving Jack his mashed carrots and tofu right about now. And Howie would be at the Croh Bar with Miriam Doncaster.

She tried his cell and got his voice mail message. Then she tried Marge, asked her to call Betty Hall and relay the message to Howie to call her as soon as possible, and set the phone down.

"You," she said to Dina. "You are a rat fink."

Dina put both hands over her face. "Do you think you should call Jerry?" she said, her voice muffled.

"Jerry Grimsby?" Quill glanced up at the clock again. The hands hadn't moved much. Why did she feel as if she'd been stuck in this kitchen filled with lunatics for hours? "Jerry's restaurant opens at seven for dinner in the summer. He'll be prepping right now."

"Maybe he can get somebody to take her some food or something. Or a file."

Clarissa Sparrow cleared her throat. "Excuse me. Jerry Grimsby? You're talking about the guy who runs L'Esperance over in Ithaca?"

Quill nodded. "He and Meg . . ." She fluttered her hand. "You know."

"He's going to be so pissed off at me," Dina mourned.

"*He* is?" Quill muttered. "I'm not exactly swinging from the chandeliers, here." Her cell phone shrilled the opening bars to "Rondo alla Turca." The little window said *Howie*. Quill picked the phone up as she said, "Go into my office, Dina. Call Bjarne and ask him to cover for Meg here in the kitchen. I'll be with you in a minute."

Howie, thank goodness, wasn't a tut-tutter. But he reminded Quill that he couldn't represent Meg himself, since he'd be the justice called upon to rule on the request for remand. "You know I've taken on a junior partner," he said. In the background, Quill heard the cheerful din that meant Happy Hour at the Croh Bar was in full swing. "His name is Justin Alvarez. I'll send him down to the clink and get things rolling."

She thanked him, shut the cell phone off, and pushed open the doors to the dining room.

One of the three parties that had made dinner reservations was already seated. Quill saw with approval that Kathleen had a tray of drinks ready for them. The couple sat at the table nearest the floor-to-ceiling windows that faced the waterfall. The part of Quill's brain that was perpetually on innkeeper alert noted that the cadet blue carpeting could probably last another year, and that the deep cream tablecloths really looked very nice with the pale violet blue of the hydrangeas that made up the centerpieces.

Quill waved to Kathleen as she passed by, then paused and greeted the dinner guests. At a guess, they were in their mid-sixties, and from the rose corsage worn by the woman, they had come to the inn for a celebration.

"Welcome to the Inn at Hemlock Falls," Quill said warmly. "Is this your first time with us?"

They nodded. "Couldn't get in at Bonne Goutè," the woman said. "And it's our fortieth wedding anniversary. Well, it's tomorrow, actually, and the kids have this big party planned, but I said to Frank, wouldn't it be nice if we had dinner, just the two of us?"

"And I said, it sure would," Frank said heartily. "Don't mind being here at all." He waved the menu at her. "It's cheaper than that Bonne Goutè place, too."

"Well," Quill said. "There is that. Kathleen, please see that a bottle of the good champagne's brought to this table will you? And take your time about deciding," she added kindly.

"Little delay in the kitchen," Kathleen offered. She was as sturdily built as her brother, but where Davy Kiddermeister was fair-haired and blushed at the drop of the hat, she was dark-haired and sallow. The only familial resemblance was their pale blue eyes. "Chef's in jail for a bit. But we've got the backup headed this way speedy quick. I'll see to that champagne, Quill."

Quill kept her smile firmly in place as she went through the archway that led from the dining room to the reception area. With luck, the promise of free champagne would keep the fortieth-anniversary couple from scooting out the front door.

Dina wasn't behind the desk. Quill hoped that meant she'd gone into the office with Clarissa Sparrow and called Bjarne. She noted that the daylilies in the two hip-high Oriental vases that flanked the reception desk were due for a change, looked askance at the spindle with its stack of pink While You Were Out messages, and opened the door to her office with the feeling that this particular day better end soon, or she was going to go stark staring bonkers.

Clarissa Sparrow stood at the window, looking out at the driveway with a hopeful expression. Dina sat on the couch. She straightened up with a guilty start as Quill came into the room and blurted, "Bjarne's on vacation this week. Until Tuesday."

"Oh, no!" Quill sat down behind her desk with a sigh. "I forgot. Oh, phooey."

"And I'm sorry about the stuff with Meg . . . you know. Ratting her out to Davy." She paused, then offered, "Your hair's falling all over a bit."

Quill's hair was always out of control, just like everything else. She pulled it on top of her head in a loose topknot when she got up in the morning, and by this time of day it was always halfway down her back. She twisted it back up and wound the scrunchie twice around the roots. "Well," she said. "Now that I can actually see, things look better."

"I'll quit if you want," Dina said. "It's just that I didn't think! I was in the middle of going over the gestation periods for my copepods and my mind was elsewhere."

"Dina's a graduate student in limnology at Cornell," Quill said in response to Clarissa's puzzled expression. "Limnology's the study of freshwater lakes, which we have plenty of around here, as you know. I don't know what copepods are."

"Lake organisms," Dina said. "A freshwater crustacean of the subclass Copepoda. I keep telling you."

"Whatever," Quill said. "Let's get back to the rat-finkery."

"Well, Davy showed up and I thought he was just, like, asking me about some gossip he'd heard, and then he made me write it out and sign it and I thought, oh, heck. I feel just awful about this! I honestly didn't mean to get Meg into trouble." Two large tears rolled down Dina's cheeks.

"It could be worse," Quill said kindly.

"How?" Dina sobbed.

"Oh, I don't know," Quill said vaguely. "We could be in the middle of a forest fire or something. Here." She pulled a tissue from the box on her desk and leaned over to hand it to Dina. "Look. I've handled the kitchen before, and Doreen is with Jack, as usual, and we only have two other bookings for dinner. So I can cope. There's just that one anniversary couple in the dining room right now. But you'll have to stay on at the reception desk, Dina. No date with Davy."

"That's only fair," Dina said eagerly. "And do you want me to make up a packet to send to Meg? Food and whatever? Some nice soap?"

Quill resisted the impulse to clutch at her hair again. "She'll be back before she needs to take a shower, I'm sure. I called Howie."

"I could give you a hand in the kitchen, if you like." Clarissa Sparrow turned away from the window. "I'm a chef."

"Oh my God," Dina said. "I almost forgot you were there. Quill, this is Clarissa Sparrow. Clarissa, this is my boss, Sarah Quilliam."

"You're a chef?" Quill said. "Of course. Is that where I've seen you before? On the tour of Bonne Goutè?" She closed her eyes, trying to remember. "You're pastry, right?" But there was something else. Clarissa wasn't beautiful, exactly, but she was distinctive. She was slim, maybe too slim, with angular cheekbones, dark hair, and, like Meg, clear gray eyes.

"Right. But I trained at CB . . . Cordon Bleu . . . and I can handle three entrees, no problem."

"That'd be just great," Quill said. "But I hate to impose." She hesitated. "Of course, we'd be glad to reimburse you for your time."

"We'll see," Clarissa said. "It's my awful boss that's put you into this situation, after all. But maybe we can talk about this in the kitchen? I'd better get started."

Quill led the way out of the office and almost collided with Kathleen in the entryway to the dining room.

"Hi, Quill, hi, Dina." Her gaze slid curiously over Clarissa Sparrow, but she said, "I've been looking for you guys. I gave the VanderMolens another bottle of champagne and a cheese plate, so they're feeling no pain, but the Adriansen party just got here and they don't drink. So they want food." She glanced over her shoulder at the party of four seated next to the wine rack. "I think they're serious eaters," she said in a whisper. "You know, foodies. They asked if we had a seasonal menu. And they're getting a little cross."

"You know what?" Clarissa said. "I can handle this. People like that came into my rest . . . that is, I'm familiar with this type of customer." She smiled. Until she'd smiled, Quill hadn't registered how sad her expression was.

"Sure," Quill said. "I'll just check things out in the kitchen. We have a small staff on Mondays, but there *is* a staff. Kathleen will give you a menu, and we list the evening specials on the blackboard. I'll wait for you in there."

Clarissa nodded and made her way gracefully past the empty tables to the Adriansens and their guests. Something, either the challenge of cooking in an unfamiliar kitchen or the chance to talk to the guests, seemed to have pulled her out of herself. In a matter of moments, she had two women in the party smiling and the men nodding self-importantly.

"Lucky she was here," Dina said. "It could have been a disaster. Not," she added hastily, "that you aren't a good cook, Quill."

"Why *is* she here, Dina?"

"Her cat. She lost her cat. Well, she didn't lose it, exactly; it ran away after M. LeVasque threw it out the back door of the cooking academy. She's put up signs down in the village and they've got that Lost, Stolen, or Strayed thing on the radio . . ."

Quill put her hand up. "Stop. Go back to the reception desk. Call upstairs and see if Doreen needs anything to eat. Jack should be fast asleep by now, but if he isn't, come and get me. Answer the phones. Take messages. Book rooms. Do your job. Stay there until the dining room closes or unless Jack needs me."

"Okay. What if I hear something about Clarissa's cat?"

Quill clapped her hand to her forehead. "The cat. Is it a big orange cat?"

"Clarissa says it's a Maine coon cat. I guess it's huge."

"Okay. I think it's under the hydrangea on the beach. Call Mike. Ask him to get a handful of liver bits from Doreen."

"Doreen has liver bits?"

"Never mind about the liver bits. Ask Mike to get Max's dog cage and ask him to go down to the beach and lure the cat into the carrier. And then Mike can bring it up to the kitchen."

"Clarissa's cat's under the hydrangea bush? I'll tell her right now! She was so worried about that cat."

"Let's see if it's still there. If it isn't, she'll be even more worried. If it is, problem solved. Let's check it out before we get her hopes up."

"Okay." Dina sighed. "I guess this means no movie with Davy, but that's okay. This is pretty much an emergency. I'll let you know if Mike finds the cat."

"Good."

Dina scanned Quill's expression and said wisely, "You want me to go away and get all this rolling."

"Sooner than now," Quill agreed.

Clarissa joined her as she walked into the kitchen.

"Think you can handle this okay?"

Clarissa smiled. "I'd say 'piece of cake' except that good cake's never easy. This will be easy."

"I hope so, for all our sakes. We've got a dishwasher and prep person on hand at the moment. I'll introduce you."

Meg recruited graduate students from the nearby Cornell School of Hotel Administration to handle the basic-skills jobs, and the two nervous kids jumped to attention as Quill and Clarissa came in.

"We heard Meg's in jail!" the girl said.

"It's Devon, isn't it?" Quill said to the tall blond boy holding a pot scrubber. She turned to the slim girl with the tomato sieve. "And you're Mallory. And yes, Meg's in jail, but she's just visiting. Like Monopoly." Quill shut her eyes briefly. Her two universes collided all the time. Mother and manager. "Never mind."

"Kathleen came in looking for a cheese plate with local stuff," Mallory said. "We put together a soft/hard sort of thing, but, Mrs. McHale, there I couldn't find anything other than the ewe's milk cheddar from downstate and some French Brie. I hope that's okay. We couldn't think of anything else to do."

"Things are fine. Meg will be out soon; in the meantime,

Chef Sparrow's in charge. Clarissa? This is Devon McAllister and Mallory DiCosta."

"You both did beautifully with the cheese plate," Clarissa said. "Now, I'm going to need both of you to help me get acquainted with this kitchen. Devon? I'll need you to prep a pasta dish, and Mallory, we're going to slap together a nice starter for table thirty-two."

Quill felt herself relax. "And I'll be right outside, if you need me."

Nobody looked up. After a few moments, Quill went out the back door and sat down on the kitchen porch. It was close to eight o'clock and a full moon was rising in the east. The air was cool, and a few clouds drifted across the twilight sky. A satisfying clink of pots and pans sang out from the kitchen. Two stories over her head, Jack was peacefully asleep.

And Myles?

She sighed. She wouldn't think about Myles.

She pulled her sketch pad from one pocket and the stub of a charcoal pencil from the other. She made a quick drawing of the cat under the hydrangea bush and set it aside. Then she checked her cell phone, in case she'd missed a message from Meg. (She hadn't.) There was a brief rustling in the rosemary bush at the front of the garden and Max emerged covered, as usual, with bits of sticks, burrs, and a variety of leaves. He sat down beside her, scratched himself vigorously, and dropped his head in her lap with a contented grunt. Quill combed his coat with her fingers and carefully teased the burrs from his ears. Her cell phone sounded.

"Hey," Meg said.

"Hey, yourself. Are you out?"

"I'm out. Davy's going to drive me back."

"Are you all right?"

Meg snorted. "It'll take a lot more than a couple of hours in stir to crack this cookie."

"Howie couldn't come himself, so he sent his junior associate. I hope it all went smoothly."

"Justin," Meg said. "Justin was great."

Quill was familiar with that note in her sister's voice. "Dina thought we might call Jerry, in case you needed anything."

"Just cool it, sis."

"Okay," Quill said amiably. "I'll see you in a few minutes, then." She slipped the cell phone back in her pocket and ruffled Max's ears. "Looks like the relationship with Jerry Grimsby is cooling off, Max. I can't say I'm surprised. Two chefs in one household—I'd call that a recipe for disaster." She nudged the sleepy dog. "Ho-ho. I'll tell you the worst thing about Myles being away, Max. No one else gets my jokes."

Max rolled one eye up at her and yawned.

"Actually," Quill said, "that's not the worst thing about Myles being away. The worst thing is sleeping by myself at night. And Myles not seeing the way Jack changes from day to day. Although I do make a quick little drawing of him, every morning, just so Myles can see where he's been and where he's going. That and the photographs."

Somebody pushed the screen door open. Max lifted his head and thumped his tail on the decking. Clarissa came out onto the porch. "Just came out to tell you things are well under control." She smiled down at Max. "That's one of the nicest things about a dog. You can talk to it any time, and it always listens."

"Cats, too," Quill said. She handed the sketch of the cat up to her.

"Bismarck!" Clarissa sat down beside her, and angled the sketch so that she could see it better in the light from the kitchen windows. "Have you seen him? Do you know where he is?"

"He was down by our little beach this afternoon. As soon

as Dina told me it might be your cat, I sent our groundskeeper down to bring him back up for you."

"Uh-oh." Clarissa got to her feet. "Bismarck has um . . .
issues. Maybe I'd better go give your guy a hand. Oh, shoot.
There's the desserts. Table twenty-seven's too drunk to
care, but the foursome's going to want berries."

"I can handle the desserts," Quill said bravely. "I'd want
to be there, myself, if it were my cat."

"It's not Bismarck I'm worried about," Clarissa said.
"Bismarck can take care of himself."

"So can Mike," Quill assured her. The sound of a car coming up the drive made her get to her feet. "And that sounds
like Meg. We're saved. She can handle the desserts."

The glare of headlights swept the small parking lot that
sat to the left of the gardens.

"She's out already?" Clarissa said. "My gosh. You guys
must have fabulous lawyers."

"One way or the other, we're pretty familiar with the
criminal justice system," Quill said. "It's more like we're
used to the routine."

Clarissa narrowed her eyes at the lights and grabbed her
wrist. "Hang on. Do you guys own a Mercedes 450 SL?"

"A what?" Quill squinted into the darkness. The lights on
the car dimmed, leaving the parking lot shrouded in moon-
light.

"That car." Clarissa's grip tightened. "That long, low-
slung shape. Your police force doesn't happen to drive Mer-
cedeses, does it?"

"Good grief. Of course not."

"Then that," Clarissa said grimly, "is not your sister."

She sprang into the kitchen and slammed the door.

5

A car door slammed and footsteps crunched in the parking lot gravel. Max stood up, his head cocked, his ears tipped forward in mild interest.

Bernard LeVasque walked out of the dark and stepped up onto the porch.

"Where is your manager?" he demanded.

Quill opened her mouth and shut it. She'd never actually met LeVasque, but she had followed in his wake at the open house, as he'd swanned around his fabulous new building. His face was mostly jaw, with little piggy eyes and thinning brown hair. Quill was good at judging ages. LeVasque's boastful bio (the first page in the elaborate and expensive brochure he distributed in every single retail establishment in Hemlock Falls) inferred he was in his mid-forties. She'd be willing to bet her best set of camel-hair brushes he was sixty, at least. He'd had some work done, as Quill's mother used to delicately phrase it. And, despite the presence of his little potbelly, it was pretty clear he worked out at a gym to help hold on to the big age lie.

"I'm Sarah Quilliam-McHale," she said pleasantly. "My sister and I are the owners here."

"The female chef." He sneered. "And you, the female boss."

Quill had been blessed with an equable temperament, so she was a little startled to realize that she was truly pissed off. She unclenched her teeth. "I take it you didn't just drop by to chat?"

"Is Clarissa Sparrow here!?" he demanded.

"Yes, she is. And I must thank you for . . ."

"You have seduced away one of my chefs. I am here to sue you," he said with relish.

"Down, Max," Quill ordered the dog, who hadn't moved at all except to wag his tail. She grabbed Max by the collar. Max wagged his tail even faster and panted happily. "I don't think I'm going to be able to hold him, M. LeVasque."

LeVasque backed up a few steps. "This dog is vicious?"

"Very," Quill said.

Max wriggled free of her hold on his collar, sat down, and scratched amiably at his neck.

"Max attacks on command," Quill said. "This dog is a Schutzhund."

LeVasque drew his scanty eyebrows together. "The Schutzhund is a breed of Alsatian bred for security work. Very fierce, no? You Americans call it a German shepherd, *peut-être*. That is not a Schutzhund. That is a mutt."

"Appearances can be deceiving, M. LeVasque."

LeVasque spat contemptuously over his left shoulder. "Yes. That is vair-y true, that appearances are deceiving. Mme. Margaret Quilliam looks like a perfectly acceptable *femme*. Instead, she is a thief as well as a *provocateur*. Now there will be a second lawsuit over the steal of my employee's services."

"I have no idea what you're talking about." Quill hoped like anything that Clarissa had made it out of the inn and was back on her way to the culinary academy. "As far as Ms. Sparrow's services are concerned, the whole concept of indentured servitude went out in the eighteenth century. And slavery was declared illegal in 1862. It's a free country and you can't," she concluded, somewhat inelegantly, "sue us for squat."

"No?" He pushed his way past her and marched into the kitchen. Quill, at his heels, was dismayed to see Clarissa chopping raw sugar into a fine powder with a butcher knife.

"Hah! I knew it!" LeVasque put both hands on his hips, jutted out his considerable jaw, and shouted, "*Nom de nom! C'est insupportable!* What are you doing here!"

"I have Monday nights off," Clarissa said coolly. "I can be anywhere I want."

M. LeVasque's eyes were little, beady, and mean. Like Napoleon, he was short. Also rude, aggressive, and militant.

"Sir," Quill said. "I do not want you in my kitchen."

"It's a free country," LeVasque said mockingly. "I can be any-wair I want." He swept Meg's kitchen with a contemptuous gaze. "And you call this a kitchen? I call this a . . . a . . . midden!"

"Hey!" Quill said. "That's just plain insulting. I really think, M. LeVasque . . ."

"You really think? Hah! Women do not think." He sucked his lower lip, then released it with a popping sound. "I tell you what. You!" He stuck his forefinger under Clarissa's nose. "Are fired. And you!" He swiveled on his feet and waved his fist in the air at Quill. "My lawyers will contact your lawyers!"

Clarissa slapped the butcher knife back in the rack, swept the sugar up in the palm of her hand, and flung it at LeVasque. Then both chefs stood nose to nose and started yelling.

Quill went to the dining room doors and peeked out.

Three of the tables were full, as expected, and two of the tables were having such a good time the place could have exploded and no one would have noticed. The anniversary couple, on the other hand, looked scared.

Quill let the doors close, turned around, and put her hands on her hips. She would have to get firm. Clarissa had succumbed to the temptation of the eight-inch sauté pan and advanced on LeVasque with murder in her eye. Le-Vasque was retreating backward around the prep table. Suddenly, Devon sprang forward, grabbed LeVasque by the collar, and propelled him toward the back door.

The screen door banged. There was a friendly farewell bark from Max the Schutzhund, and LeVasque was gone.

The screen door banged again, and Quill grabbed the eight-inch sauté pan out of Clarissa's hand, in case LeVasque was back. It wasn't LeVasque; it was Mike Santini, the guy who kept the gardens and grounds in such wonderful shape, and Quill had never been so glad to see anyone in all her life. He was small and wiry and tough as an old boot. He'd settle LeVasque's hash in two seconds flat.

"Hey, Mike."

"Hey." He kept a wary eye on the sauté pan in her hand. "I thought Meg was in jail."

"She's out. She should be back any minute." Quill looked dubiously at the pan and hung it back up. Then she sat down in the rocking chair and buried her head in her hands. "Yikes. I can't believe I did that."

"LeVasque has that effect on people," Clarissa said. "I'm sorry."

"You're sorry? You work for that monster. I'm sorry for you!"

"Yeah, well, I don't have a lot of choice, do I?" Clarissa looked at Mike with a smile. "You wouldn't be the Mike that went after my cat, by any chance?"

"That sucker belong to you?" He shook his head admiringly. "Whoo. That's some beauty."

"You have him then?" Clarissa asked. "He didn't hurt you, did he?"

Mike rubbed the back of his neck. "I don't have him, exactly, no."

"Oh, no!"

"I almost had him." He looked at Quill. "I did what you suggested, Boss. I got some of those liver bits of off Doreen and took Max's carrier down to the river. And he was like, half in the bag, so to speak, when you know who shows up."

"You know who?" Quill said, bewildered.

"Carol Ann Spinoza." He rubbed the back of his neck with both hands. "And that cat? That cat don't like Carol Ann Spinoza one little bit. So the cat, like, growls at her and sort of shows his teeth like this." Mike drew his lips back in a horrible grimace. "And Carol Ann Spinoza screams like a banshee. So the cat goes flying off somewheres. But not," he added with satisfaction, "until he, like, bites her a good one on the ankle. So." He shrugged. "I don't have that cat."

Quill clutched at her hair, which was coming down from her top knot again.

"Is this Carol Ann very hurt?" Clarissa asked.

"Nah. She had boots on."

"Boots? Who wears boots in August?"

"Carol Ann," Quill said glumly. "They're part of the uniform. Carol Ann's the animal control officer."

"Thank goodness."

Quill exchanged rueful glances with Mike and said, "Don't thank goodness too soon."

"But that's a good thing, isn't it? I mean, animal control people are experts at catching pets safely."

"She's more likely to shoot it," Mike said. "Or poison it. Or run it over with her animal control Jeep. That Carol Ann's damn mean."

"Shoot Bismarck!" Clarissa said. "She can't do that."

"Not at night, that's for sure," Mike said. "Sheriff's department took away her infrared rifle."

Quill relaxed a little. Clarissa looked even more alarmed.

The screen door banged a third time. Quill was beginning to feel she was in the middle of the second act of *Noises Off*.

Meg came into the kitchen looking so chipper Quill wanted to smack her just on principle. "Hey, guys!" she said. "Is this party just for me?" She spread her arms wide. "Free at last!" She caught sight of Clarissa and cocked her head, just like Max. "Gosh, don't I know you?"

"I'm Clarissa Sparrow."

"From Bonne Goutè. Sure! You're pastry, right? From all I hear, I should take a couple of lessons from you."

Quill stared at her sister in astonishment. Meg had many, many fine character traits, but she was competitive to the bone.

"The secret's in the butter. Irish butter." Clarissa extended her hand and Meg shook it. "I was pinch-hitting in the kitchen while you were . . ." She trailed off.

"In the pokey," Meg said cheerfully. "Quill left a message that the cooking was taken care of. We're lucky you were available."

"Yes. Well, it was a privilege. It was just a fluke I was here. I was out looking for my cat."

"Big orange cat?" Meg said. "There's a big orange cat sitting out in the parking lot."

"Oh, my!" Clarissa said. "Excuse me, will you?" She grabbed her backpack from under the prep sink and took out a collar and leash. On her way out the door, she said, "Those blueberries? They're for table forty-two. I was going to add mascarpone, chopped raw sugar, and a little shortcake. Cake's cooling on top of the Viking."

Meg went to the stove, broke off a piece of the shortcake, and tasted it. Then she looked very thoughtful. "Terrific," she said, absently. "Sensational, in fact. I've only tasted something like this once before."

"Clarissa said it's her standby," Devon offered. "Berries, mascarpone, and a little garnish. All-purpose summer dessert."

"Little lemon, maybe," Meg said. She bent over and inspected the blueberries. "Devon, you can handle this. Add a slice of lemon and some of the fresh mint for garnish. Then plate it and send it out to the dining room."

Devon went obediently to the stove and picked up the pan of shortcake.

Meg looked at the clock over the fireplace. "Shoot. Only eight thirty. I suppose I'd better get back to work."

"Did you have a good time in jail?" Quill asked sarcastically.

"I had an excellent time."

Quill sat up and took a deep breath. "You must be drunk. Or exhausted. I don't care if it is early. We're going to close the kitchen. Mike, please go and tell Kathleen not to seat any walk-ins. And thank you for trying to rescue the cat."

"Anytime," Mike said laconically. "And if there's nothing else except to give that message to Kath, I'll be off home."

"Nothing else." She waited until Mike had disappeared into the dining room and then grabbed her sister's arm. "He came back."

"Who came back?" Meg's eyes widened. "LeVasque came back?"

"Big as life and twice as ugly," Quill said. "He found out Clarissa was here, taking over for you in the kitchen."

"And?"

"And he fired her."

"Golly." Meg ran her hands through her hair, which was short, dark, and tended to stick up like a little kid's if she didn't pay attention. "She's well out of it, is my guess. The guy's a total creep."

Quill winced at yet another slam of the screen door. Operant conditioning, that's what it was called. You were given a negative stimulus over and over until you were ready to scream when it jabbed you again.

"You okay?"

"I keep thinking it's LeVasque."

"It's not. Just me." Clarissa edged her way into the kitchen. Her arms were full of cat. "I brought Bismarck in to say thank you."

There was a lot of Bismarck, and he obscured most of Clarissa's upper torso. He blinked placidly and then, as Max trotted in behind Clarissa, extended a giant paw down to the dog and flexed his claws. Max gave the cat a quick glance and shot through the doors to the dining room.

"Sorry," Clarissa said.

"He's gone up to sleep with Jack," Meg said. "But that's some cat, all right."

"Is Bismarck usually an outdoor cat?" Quill asked. "If so, you might think about keeping him inside for a while. If Carol Ann's on his case, we might have a problem."

"Carol Ann's after that cat?" Meg shook her head. "That woman's a menace. Quill's right. You should think about keeping him inside."

"I usually do."

"Did he slip out the door when no one was looking?" Meg said sympathetically. "How did he get lost in the first place?"

"Bernard," Clarissa said briefly. "I told him I had a cat when he hired me, and he said"—she stuck out her lower lip and adopted a pretty good French accent—"But of course! *Le chat domestique.* What could be more French?' And of course," she continued with some bitterness, "*that* attitude lasted about a week."

"So he threw him outdoors deliberately?" Meg shook her head. "What an ass."

"Anyway," Quill interrupted. "I'm really glad everything turned out okay and that you got Bismarck back."

"Me, too. Well." Clarissa shifted the cat in her arms. "Thank you for everything. I'd better be off now."

"Off where?" Meg said bluntly.

Clarissa bit her lower lip.

"You guys are all housed at the academy, right? In that annex next to the big building?"

"Yeah. We are."

"And do you really think LeVasque's going to let you back in your apartment?" Meg turned to her sister. "You said LeVasque fired her."

"He sure did," Quill said. "Does he make a habit of it? Or did he mean it?"

"He meant it, all right," Clarissa said. "We've butted heads often enough, but he's one of those people whose word is his bond, if you know what I mean."

"I do," Quill said sympathetically.

Meg pressed on ruthlessly. "So you go back to the annex and what do you think the odds are that all your stuff will be out on the sidewalk?"

"Pretty good," Clarissa said with a laugh. "But he has to let me keep my stuff. In any event, it's my problem, not yours. I can handle it."

Meg folded her arms across her chest. "What about your recipes?"

Clarissa paled.

"Right," Meg said grimly. "What if he gets his slimy little hands on those?"

"They're on my laptop," Clarissa said. "And they're password protected." Her eyes got suspiciously bright. "He wouldn't dare. He wouldn't dare!"

Meg looked at Quill. "Are you thinking what I'm thinking?"

Quill hadn't a clue, but she nodded anyway. What she did know was that Meg didn't trust anybody with the complete list of ingredients to five or six of her most famous dishes. Not even Quill herself. And Meg would stop just short of murder if anyone tried to steal her recipes.

"Tell you what, Clarissa," Meg said. "We'll follow you over to the annex and see that everything's okay. If not, well, we'll take it from there."

Clarissa hesitated.

Meg slung her purse over her shoulder with a purposeful air. "Is that your Ford Escort out in the parking lot? I thought so. We'll take Quill's Honda." She eyed Bismarck, who was staring at her with a sort of benign malevolence. "Tell you what, though. You can take the cat."

6

~Socca~
For six personnes

⅔ cup chickpea flour
2 tablespoons LeVasque Extra Virgin Olive Oil*
½ teaspoon salt
1 cup water

Mix all ingredients and let stand one hour to allow the flour to absorb all. Heat oven to 400 degrees. Oil crepe pan, pour on the pancake mixture, and place in oven for five minutes. Remove, flip the pancake, and sprinkle olive oil attractively over the top. Replace pan in oven for five more minutes. Serve with salt and pepper.

LeVasque Extra Virgin Olive Oil is to be found in fine grocery stores everywhere.
—From *Brilliance in the Kitchen*, B. LeVasque

"You're up to something," Quill said, as she followed Clarissa's battered Escort down the winding drive from the Inn to the village. "You want to clue me in now? Or let me sit here in a state of terror?"

"Terror's good," Meg said. "I don't know that you'll approve, exactly."

"Try me."

"Does Clarissa look at all familiar?"

"I saw her when we took the tour of the academy."

"Anywhere else?"

"Meg, for Pete's sake . . . darn!" Quill braked behind Clarissa at the only red light in town, which was at the intersection of Main and Hemlock Drive. She looked both ways up and down the street. At nine o'clock on a Monday night, there wasn't much happening in Hemlock Falls. All of the wheelbarrows, lawnmowers, ladders, and buckets had been taken in from the sidewalk in front of Nickerson's Hardware. There wasn't much happening at the Croh Bar, either, since those villagers who did eat dinner out ate at six o'clock and went home to catch *American Idol*. The small businesses like Schmidt Realty and Casualty Insurance were closed until morning. The wrought-iron streetlights illuminated empty sidewalks, and the occasional raccoon foraging in the white painted planters. Almost all the buildings on Main Street were made of stone, which delighted tourists in the daytime, but gave the place the feel of a cemetery at night.

Clarissa gunned through the red light and took off down the road.

"Worried about the recipes, I think," Meg said. "Can't say as I blame her."

Quill went through the red light, too.

The Bonne Goutè Culinary Academy lay past Peterson Park between the Hemlock Falls Resort and the edge of the village. The main building was easily accessible from the road, with a long circular drive. Small, single-lane roads led off from it at intervals, much like a European roundabout. The first lane led out of the parking lot, the second into the lot, and the third to the annex, where Bernard LeVasque housed his chefs and instructors.

The annex was designed with the same white clapboard, green trim, and exquisitely polished pine decking as the larger building. Floodlights at the north and south ends of the roof illuminated the paths and lawns, without glaring directly into the apartment windows. The shrubs around the foundation were neatly trimmed and healthy. A large urn spilled white petunias over the front steps. Clarissa slammed to a halt at the portico that sheltered the entrance and killed the lights on the Escort.

"Better park facing the road," Meg said. "Just in case."

"Why do I feel guilty?" Quill said, as she followed Meg's suggestion. "We aren't breaking any laws."

"Not yet," Meg said. "Might be a good idea to turn the headlights off, too."

Quill did that. Then they both sat for a moment. The engine ticked over. Somebody in one of the apartments had the TV on; Quill heard the familiar opening of the ten o'clock news.

Clarissa got out of her car and went inside the annex. Meg poked Quill in the ribs. "You ready?"

"Ready," Quill said firmly. "Why are we whispering?"

"Why not?"

They found Clarissa in the foyer. It was spacious, perhaps twenty by twenty. A row of mailboxes was fixed on the south wall. Quill counted ten. So there must be ten apartments, five to the left and five to the right. Unless there was a laundry room.

Quill pinched herself so that she'd stop obsessing about the layout of the building. A row of brass coat hooks with a shelf underneath for boots took up the wall opposite. The floor was carpeted in the kind of indoor-outdoor carpeting that always smelled funny to Quill; rubbery, with a chemical undertone. The pattern was an inoffensive green, brown, and cream plaid.

Clarissa was taking deep, regular breaths, which, when

Quill thought about it, was a less painful way to de-stress yourself than pinching. She'd have to remember that.

"I'm in number eight," Clarissa said. "I didn't get a corner unit. Those go to the chefs with more seniority. It's just down here."

The carpeting kept their movements quiet, for which Quill was grateful.

"Damn!" Clarissa said. "Will you look at what that turkey did!"

Two four-by-four pine boards were nailed across the door to number eight.

"Madame's going to be royally pissed," Clarissa muttered. "He nailed those boards right into the door frame."

"You're locked out of your apartment and you're worried about Mrs. LeVasque being pissed?" Meg said.

Clarissa pried at the boards with her fingers. "It's not even nails. That sucker went and got a drill and put screws in here."

"Crow bar," Quill suggested. "I think there's one in the trunk. From the time Marge and I had to get into what's-his-name's trailer," she said to Meg.

Meg shook her head. "That was before I used it to get into MacAvoy's nudie bar. I didn't put it back."

The door to number seven, which was directly across from Clarissa's, opened up and a sturdy woman of about forty looked out into the hall. She had freckles, brown eyes, and hair that nature had intended to be red. Her hair had received some inexpert assistance in staying that way.

"Clarissa!" she said. "Oh my God. Are you all right?!"

"Hello, Raleigh. Raleigh, this is Quill. And her sister, Margaret Quilliam."

A smile lit her face. "*The* Margaret Quilliam? As in Shrimp Quilliam?"

"And Pork Soup Quilliam," Meg admitted in a self-deprecating way.

Clarissa, Meg, and Raleigh all chuckled, as if at a well-known joke.

"Pork soup?" Quill said. "I've never had your pork soup."

"You never had my pork soup because it's a famous disaster."

"The Shrimp Quilliam, though!" Raleigh kissed her fingers in Gallic-style appreciation and then seemed to realize they weren't there for a social call. She cast a worried look up and down the hallway. "Why don't you come in? Just for a minute. He said he'd be back. He means to post a guard at the door all night. You don't have much time." She stepped back and let the others into the room.

The apartment was quite pleasant, although the dark-veneered furniture gave it the feel of a hotel. The carpeting was beige, the walls were painted beige, and the curtains drawn over the double doors to the patio were beige, too. A reproduction of the Woodstock poster hung over the three-cushion couch and a ceramic pot of daisies sat on the bookshelf.

"You're Sarah Quilliam," Raleigh said. "The artist?"

Quill nodded. She couldn't think of a famous art disaster to fend off the admiration, so she said awkwardly, "Your rooms are very nice."

"All these places are exactly the same. I haven't had time to put any of my personal stuff in it."

"It looks very comfortable, and that's the main thing."

"It's not very comfortable at the moment," Raleigh said frankly. "Not with the Maitre on the warpath. What in the name of God is going on, Clarissa?"

"I got fired."

"Oh." Raleigh sank down on the couch. "I suppose it was only a matter of time. Wow. Wow." She looked up at them. "What are you going to do?"

"First thing is to get my recipes back." Clarissa crossed her arms, hugging herself, and began to pace up and down the room. "That little creep can't hold on to them. They're my personal property."

"The recipes are intellectual property," Meg said, with the annoying air of someone who knows something you don't. "And they're incredibly valuable. I know someone who can get them back for you but . . ."

"All LeVasque has to do is copy them," Clarissa said. "And then I'm screwed for sure."

Quill poked her sister. "Who do you know that can get them back, Meg?"

"A very good lawyer," Meg said loftily.

"And how do you know recipes are . . . what was the phrase? Intellectual property?"

"As I said. A very good lawyer told me."

"It wouldn't be this Justin Whosis. This associate Howie Murchison's taken on, by any chance."

"It might." Meg flashed her a grin. "And I have a feeling we're going to need a really good . . ."

"Ssst!" Raleigh jumped up from the couch in alarm. "Hear that?"

The building was too solidly built to shake, but there was some sort of thumping and marching around in the hall. Then someone pounded on Raleigh's door.

"Into the bedroom!" Raleigh hissed. "I'll tell him I don't know a thing."

"Not the bedroom," Meg said. "He knows we're here. Our cars are out front. And, excuse me, Clarissa, that car of yours is so ratty that it can't be mistaken for anyone else's. We'll go out that way." She pointed dramatically at the patio doors.

"Raleigh Brewster!*Ouvrez!!*"

"What the hell?" Raleigh muttered.

"He means open up," Quill said.

"Raah-leee?" shrieked a feminine voice.

"And that's Madame," Clarissa said. "She's worse than the Maitre."

Quill slung her purse over her shoulder purposefully. "And I'm with Meg. We should leave. Come on, Clarissa. We'll meet you back at the Inn."

"Ouvrez! Maintenant! Tout de suite!"

"I'll be right there," Raleigh called sweetly. "I just have to get some clothes on! I am totally naked, Madame."

There was a decided pause in the pounding at her door. Quill grabbed Clarissa's elbow and gave Meg a hearty shove toward the patio. Raleigh slid the doors open, and the three of them tumbled out onto the lawn.

"The Inn!" Quill said. "Ten minutes!"

She and Meg made a dead run for the Honda and pulled out of the driveway just as LeVasque fell through the entrance door, tripped up, Quill surmised, by the profusely apologetic Raleigh. A big guy in a nondescript gray uniform made a halfhearted lunge at Clarissa, who neatly evaded him. She tumbled into the Escort. The security guard opened the passenger door, leaned forward, and then leaped back with a shout, nursing his left hand.

"Bismarck strikes again," Quill said. "Ha!"

"Will you step on it, please?" Meg said. "I think that guy has a gun." She pulled out her cell phone. Quill, concentrating on making the turn back onto Main Street at fifty miles an hour, spared her a glance.

"What are you doing?!"

"Hey!" Meg said into the cell. "Dina? Yeah. It's me. No, I'm not mad. No, it's okay. Really. I know how sorry you are. More to the point, I know how foggy you get when you're studying your copepods. Look. You've got to give Davy a call and get him down here right away. Huh? Oh. The culinary academy. The annex. M. LeVasque's in the process of breaking and entering into a private residence. Huh? Just do it. Please. He's doing it right now!" She snapped the cell phone shut and stuck it back in her purse. "Where's Clarissa?"

Quill looked in the rearview mirror. The Escort's head-